# PEPE
## takes a Tumble!

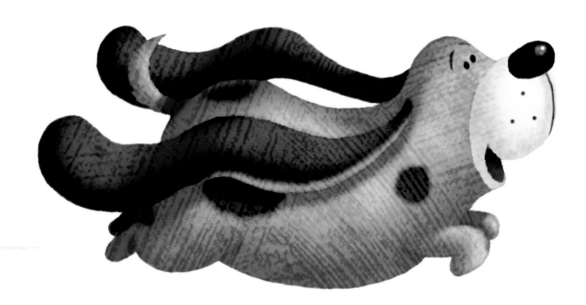

# Kes Gray & Mary McQuillan

Hodder
Children's
Books

A division of Hachette Children's Books

# Hello! I'm Nurse Nibbles,

and these are my get well friends.

Please return/renew this item by the last date shown. Books may also be renewed by telephoning, writing to or calling in at any of our libraries or on the internet.

Northamptonshire Libraries and Information Service

**Northamptonshire
County Council**

www.library.northamptonshire.gov.uk/catalogue

Zoe the Zebra

Pedro the Penguin

Chesney the Cheetah

Sonia the
Snow Rabbit

Paul the Python

First published in 2013 by Hodder Children's Books
Copyright © Get Well Friends Ltd.

# WWW.GETWELLFRIENDS.COM

Hodder Children's Books, 338 Euston Road, London, NW1 3BH
Hodder Children's Books Australia, Level 17/207 Kent Street, Sydney, NSW 2000

The right of Kes Gray to be identified as the author and Mary McQuillan as the illustrator
of this Work has been asserted by them in accordance with the Copyright, Designs and Patents Act 1988.

A catalogue record of this book is available from the British Library.

ISBN: 9781 444 90031 6

Hodder Children's Books is a division of Hachette Children's Books
An Hachette UK Company
www.hachette.co.uk

In my children's ward I have lots of comfy beds of ALL shapes and sizes.

Which is a good job, because poorly animals come to visit me from all over the world!

This morning a new little patient came to see me. His name was Pepe the puppy and he was looking very shaky indeed!

This is the story of how Pepe the puppy took a tumble.

Pepe had made a very
# big decision.

He wasn't going to be a puppy anymore.

Being a puppy was such a babyish thing to be.

From now on, Pepe the puppy was
going to be a big grown-up dog!

Pepe had been watching
grown-up dogs for ages.

He had watched grown-up
dogs weeing up trees.

He had watched grown-up
dogs chasing rabbits.

He had watched
grown-up dogs
burying bones,

and sniffing other dogs' botties.

Pepe was absolutely certain he could wee up trees and chase rabbits and bury bones and sniff other dogs' botties just as well as any grown-up dog could.

And today, he was
going to prove it
BIG TIME!

Pepe lifted his nose as high
in the air as he could, and
tiptoed into the meadow.

Holding his head up and walking on tiptoe made Pepe feel ten times bigger.

Pepe climbed to the top of the hill,
looked down and wagged his tail happily.

Looking down from a very high place
made him feel a hundred times bigger!

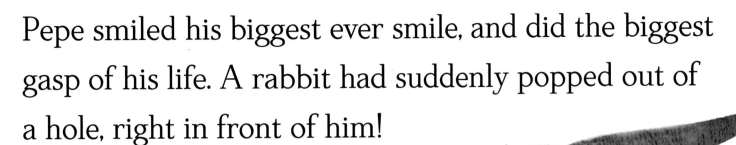

Pepe smiled his biggest ever smile, and did the biggest
gasp of his life. A rabbit had suddenly popped out of
a hole, right in front of him!

Not just any rabbit either. It was a BIG rabbit!
This was Pepe's BIG chance to show the world
what a big dog he had become.

Pepe's heart began to pound and his pulse began to race.
Not only was he going to chase that rabbit!
He was going to CATCH that rabbit!

He lowered his shoulders to the ground and crept
through the grass like a great big wolf.
He darkened his eyes like a huge man-eating shark.
He bared his teeth like a giant dinosaur.

And then he leapt at the rabbit
with a 'yap!'...

...tripped over his ears,

somersaulted through the air...

...landed on his head,
and then tumbled all
the way down to the
bottom of the hill.

Poor little Pepe.
His ears had let
him down big time!

Never mind, Pepe was a very big dog when it came to taking his medicine. He let me put cream on his bruises and bandages on his bumps.

He put on a big brave
face when his friends
came to visit him.

And I'm very pleased to tell you that
Pepe the puppy did get better in...

... THE END!

Emo the Elephant

Beyonce the Bear

Nurse Nibbles

Pepe the Puppy

Giselle the Giraffe

Momo the Monkey

# A Library Book for Bear

Bonny Becker

*illustrated by*
Kady MacDonald Denton

WALKER BOOKS
AND SUBSIDIARIES
LONDON • BOSTON • SYDNEY • AUCKLAND

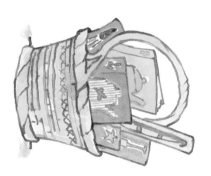

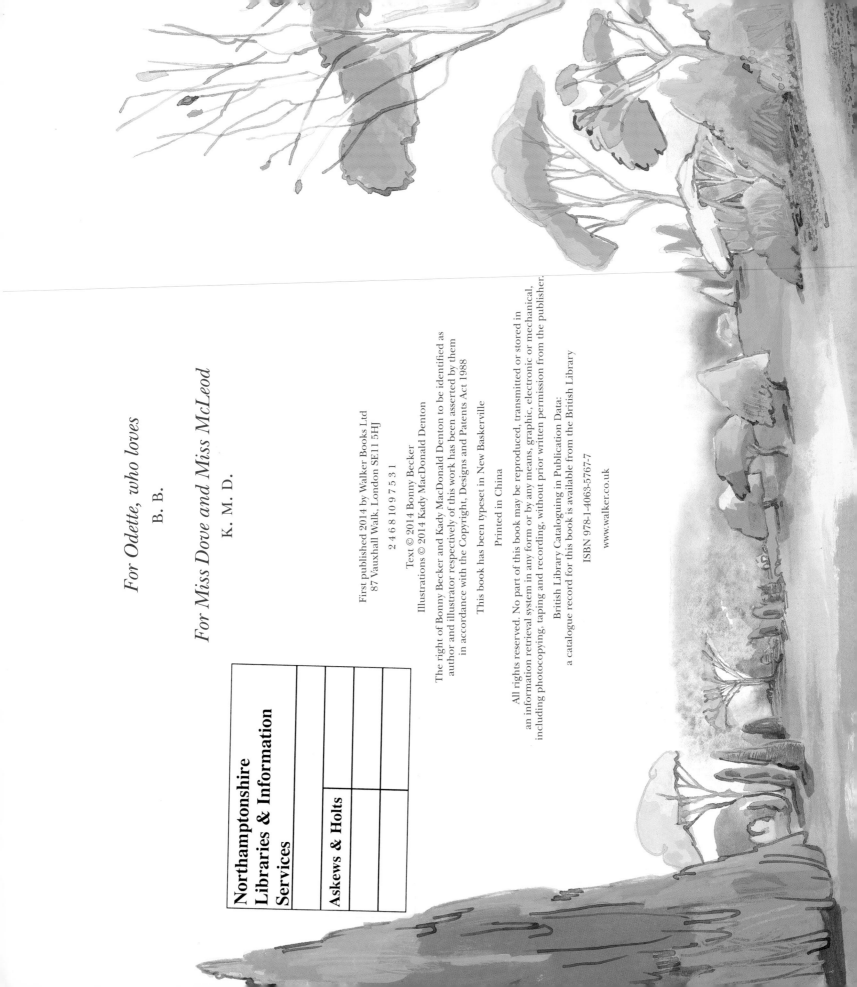

*For Odette, who loves*
B. B.

*For Miss Dove and Miss McLeod*
K. M. D.

First published 2014 by Walker Books Ltd
87 Vauxhall Walk, London SE11 5HJ

2 4 6 8 10 9 7 5 3 1

Text © 2014 Bonny Becker
Illustrations © 2014 Kady MacDonald Denton

The right of Bonny Becker and Kady MacDonald Denton to be identified as author and illustrator respectively of this work has been asserted by them in accordance with the Copyright, Designs and Patents Act 1988

This book has been typeset in New Baskerville

Printed in China

British Library Cataloguing in Publication Data:
a catalogue record for this book is available from the British Library

ISBN 978-1-4063-5767-7

www.walker.co.uk

Bear had never been to the library.

He had seven very nice books at home:

three about kings and queens, three about honey-bees

and one about pickles.

Bear was quite sure he had

all the books he would ever need.

One morning, Bear heard a *tap, tap, tapping* on his door.

When he opened the door, there was Mouse, small and grey and bright-eyed.

"We're off!" exclaimed Mouse with a happy wag of his whiskers.

Bear frowned. He had agreed to go with Mouse to the library, but now

he was quite sure it was a dreadful mistake.

"Completely unnecessary," Bear announced. "I have all the books I need right here."

"Oh, there are many delightful books in the library," Mouse assured him.

"Hmmph!" Bear grumbled – but he *had* promised.

So he buckled up his red roller skates and stepped outside, grabbing a basket for the books.

Bear skated and Mouse rode in the basket to the library, the wind rippling nicely through their fur.

But when they got to the library, Bear thought it looked much too big. "There are far too many books in there," he protested. "Most excessive!"

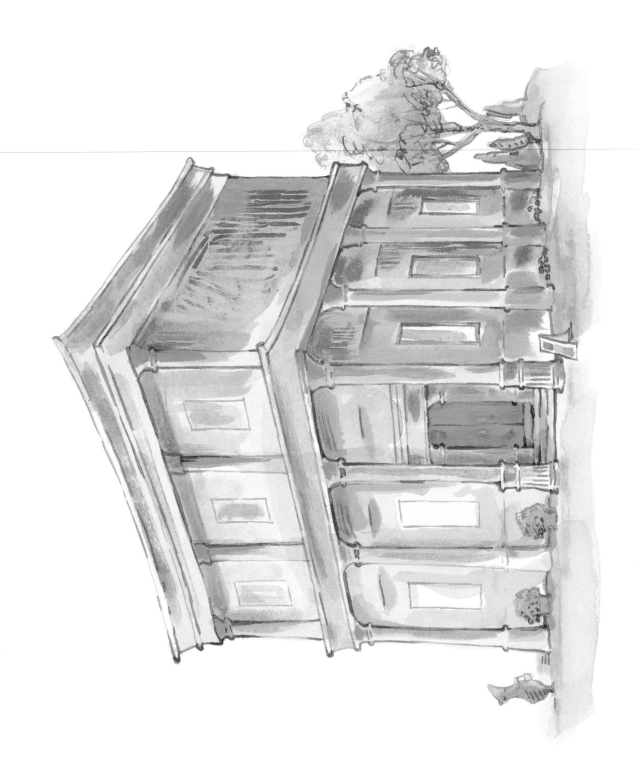

"Oh, no. It's quite exciting," Mouse said, leading Bear through the tall doors.

In the library were more books than Bear had ever thought there could be.

He quickly found a tucked-away corner. But even here, there were lots and lots of books.

"Hmmph! Terribly extravagant!" Bear's voice was a little loud.

"I shall find you the perfect one," Mouse said quietly in his library voice.

"One about pickles," commanded Bear. After all, he had only one of those.

But Mouse had whisked away.

Mouse came back with a thick green book. Bear opened it.

"Rocket ships! Ridiculous!" Bear's voice was getting louder. "A good book about pickles is all I require!"

"Remember – quiet in the library," murmured Mouse as he scurried off.

He soon returned with a tall yellow book.

"I am not interested in wooden canoes!"

Bear's voice was even louder.

"Quiet voices in the library," Mouse reminded him.

"My voice is always quiet," Bear shouted. "I will find my own book. I can assure you that pickles are quite interesting!"

Mouse didn't look so sure. But Bear quickly spotted a blue book with a pickle on the spine, and Mouse sprang up to the shelf to get it for him.

Inside were pictures of pickles. The pickles had little fairy wings.

They were dancing with petunias.

**"NO DANCING PICKLES!"** Bear roared.

**"SHHHHHHHH!"** said a voice.

Bear peeked round a bookshelf.

There sat a librarian with a cluster of youngsters gathered around her.
The librarian smiled, but a mother squirrel squished an angry finger
against her lips, and an old raccoon said sternly, "Quiet in the library."

Bear turned back with a huffy sniff. "I know when
I'm not wanted," he told Mouse. "I want to go home."

"Surely, at least one book—" Mouse began.

But Bear cut him off: "I have all the books I need."

He looked quite certain.

"Then we're off," said Mouse, but his whiskers didn't wag this time.

Bear stood stock-still. He was listening carefully to a

voice on the other side of the bookshelf.

"So the Very Brave Bear began to inch his way towards the treasure chest…"

the voice was saying.

"I'm ready—" began Mouse.

"**SHHHHHHHH!**" exclaimed Bear.

"It's just getting to the good part!"

"But you said—"

# "QUIET VOICES IN THE LIBRARY!"

Bear bellowed.

This time the librarian got up and looked round the bookshelf at Bear.

Bear stood very still and quiet, as if he had been still and quiet all along.

"Would you like to join story time?" the librarian asked.

Bear glanced at Mouse.

"We'd love to have you," said the librarian.

Bear and Mouse scooted round the shelf and found two empty chairs.

The librarian began to read again.

"Bear lifted the lid of the treasure chest, and inside…"

The librarian paused. Mouse and Bear strained forwards.

"Inside," she said, "was a mound of pickle slices. And each shining slice was made of diamonds and gold! And everyone shouted, 'Hooray for the Very Brave Bear!'"

And then she said, "The end."

Bear stared dreamily into space for a moment. Then he looked over at Mouse and announced, "As I said, pickles are most interesting."

"Indeed," said Mouse.

Later, Mouse rode in the basket with seven new books. There were two about wooden canoes, two about rocket ships, two about teapots …

and one called *The Very Brave Bear and the Treasure of Pickle Island*, which Bear read to Mouse that very same day.